In Trouble with **Bertie Barker**

For Reuben
R.I.

For Ted
M.W.

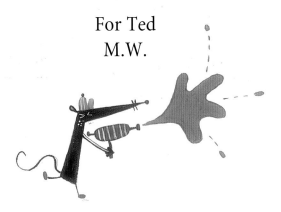

Reading Consultant: Prue Goodwin, Lecturer in literacy and children's books

ORCHARD BOOKS
338 Euston Road, London NW1 3BH
Orchard Books Australia
Hachette Children's Books
Level 17/207 Kent Street, Sydney NSW 2000

First published in 2010 by Orchard Books
First paperback publication in 2011

Text © Rose Impey 2010
Illustrations © Melanie Williamson 2010

ISBN 978 1 40830 218 7 (hardback)
ISBN 978 1 40830 226 2 (paperback)

1 3 5 7 9 10 8 6 4 2 (hardback)
1 3 5 7 9 10 8 6 4 2 (paperback)

Printed in China

Orchard Books is a division of Hachette Children's Books,
an Hachette UK company.

www.hachette.co.uk

Nipper McFee

In Trouble with **Bertie Barker**

Written by ROSE IMPEY

Illustrated by MELANIE WILLIAMSON

ORCHARD BOOKS

Nipper McFee was in trouble again!
And this time it was a double helping.

This time trouble was wearing
matching pink T-shirts that said:
I'm a little angel.
But they weren't angels. Nipper
called his sisters: *double trouble.*

"I want to spring-clean the
flat today," Mrs McFee told Nipper.
"And I want you to look after
Mimi and Fifi."
"Why can't Monty do it?" Nipper
moaned.

But Nipper's brother, Monty,
was far too busy – being perfect.
Being perfect took a lot of practice.

Keeping out of trouble took
a lot of practice, too.
And today Nipper was going
to get plenty of it.

Nipper was already in a bad mood.
His friends, Will and Lil, were going
on a trip to the Wild Cats Safari Park.
Nipper wanted to go with them.

Instead he was stuck with the twins who never stopped moaning.

We're bored!

But even bigger trouble was on its way.

Nipper's enemies, the basement rats,
had spotted him. They chased after
him with their usual cry, "Get Nipper!"

Nipper tried to make a quick escape,
but the twins wouldn't budge.
"I've got a stone in my shoe,"
moaned Mimi.
"I've got a stitch in my side,"
groaned Fifi.

Slowed down by his sisters,
Nipper was a sitting target
for the rats.

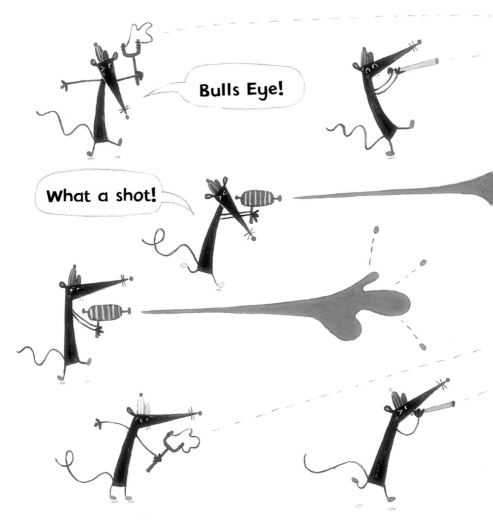

They prepared their ammunition and took aim – with peashooters, and water pistols and catapults.

Got him!

Nipper promised the twins a ride at the funfair – if only they would move a bit faster.

"Two rides!" said Mimi.

"And some candyfloss!" said Fifi.

"*Anything,*" agreed Nipper.

Magically the twins moved like lightning.

FAIR

At last Nipper had lost those
pesky rats. But his pesky sisters
were still driving him mad.

"You promised us a ride," said Fifi.

"*Two* rides," said Mimi.
It cost Nipper most of
his pocket money. "Anything
for a quiet life," he thought.

But it wasn't quiet for long.
Those rotten rodents had found
him again. Now they were pelting
Nipper with acorns and conkers.

Nipper was fizzing mad.

It was time for revenge – and

Nipper had the perfect plan.

Nipper waited for Bertie Barker, the man who ran the merry-go-round, to go for a cup of tea.
He told Mimi and Fifi, "Stay there, and don't move."

Then Nipper jumped onto the ride
and called to the rats, "Catch me
if you can!"

The rats didn't need telling twice.
"*Get Nipper!*" they cried as they
raced onto the merry-go-round.

But Nipper had disappeared.
The rats couldn't find him anywhere.

25

Before they could turn around,
Nipper started the ride.
He put it on *extra-extra-fast.*

The rats felt as if they were in the
fast spin of a washing machine.
They clung on for dear life, too
scared to get off!

When Bertie Barker came back
he was *furious.*
He blamed it all on the rats.
When he stopped the ride, the rats
fell off. But they were all too dizzy
to run away.

nee noor... nee noor... nee noor...

PC Poodle came to arrest them.

Nipper couldn't help smiling.

He had shown those rats, yet again,

not to mess with Nipper!

Nipper bought Mimi and Fifi
a big stick of candyfloss each.
Now he had spent *all* his pocket
money, but Nipper didn't mind.